Rabén & Sjögren Bokförlag, Stockholm
www.raben.se

Originally published in Sweden by Rabén & Sjögren under the title *Jamen Benny*

Library of Congress Control Number: 2001089554
Printed in Denmark
First American edition, 2002
ISBN 91-29-65497-1

Barbro Lindgren • Olof Landström

Benny and the Binky

Translated by
Elisabeth Kallick Dyssegaard

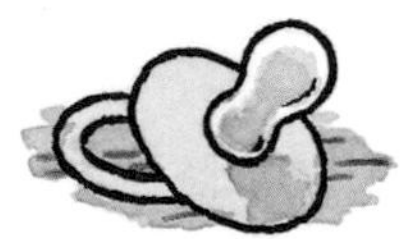

Stockholm New York London Adelaide Toronto

Benny has a brother now.
He wanted one. And then he got one.

One morning when he woke up, his brother was lying next to him.

"Benny, you have a brother," said Benny's mama.
"Yes, I know," said Benny.

Benny's brother screams and screams. Benny's mama gets a binky.

“I want a binky, too,” says Benny.
But he doesn’t get one.
“You are too big for a binky,” says Benny’s mama.
“No, I’m not,” says Benny.

All day long, little brother sucks on his binky. Benny doesn't get to try it. He is already tired of his little brother. He'd rather have the binky.

“I’m going out with little brother,” he says to his mama.
But she doesn’t hear.

Benny puts his little brother outside the door.
Then he takes the binky.
His little brother gets Little Piggy instead.

Then Benny runs away.

He runs by several houses. He is happy. The binky is good.

Benny runs by a day-care center.
"You're too big for a binky!" shout the kids.
"No, I'm not!" shouts Benny.

Later, he meets three tough pigs with soccer shoes.
"What kind of oddball is this with a binky?" ask the tough pigs.

"My name is Benny," says Benny.
"Let's punch him in the snout," say the tough pigs.

Benny is scared. He runs for his life.

But the tough pigs run after him.
Benny has his usual feet, but the tough pigs have soccer shoes!

They catch him easy as can be. The toughest one hits him on the snout, so the binky flies out.

Then a dog that Benny knows comes by.
"They took my binky," says Benny, crying.

The dog yells at the tough pigs.
"Hand over the binky before I bite your knuckles off," says the dog.

The tough pigs get very scared.
They hand over the binky right away.
Then a loud cry can be heard. It is Benny's little brother.
He's tired of Little Piggy.

Benny runs as fast as he can.

But when his little brother gets the binky back, he's happy again.

Benny goes around the house with his little brother.

Then they go back inside.

"Oh, Benny," says Benny's mama. "How nice of you to take your little brother outside!"